Contents

1 Going Fishing

My hour of cartoon heaven came to an abrupt end with the sound of hooves clip-clopping across the paved yard. Mom, Dad, and my older sister Clare were back from doing the herding. They'd be in for breakfast in a matter of minutes; just as long as it took to untack their horses and feed them. I snuggled down for a final time under my warm quilt in the armchair in our sitting-room and waited for my peace to be broken.

Suddenly an alarm-bell sounded in my head. I leapt to my feet.

'It's Saturday. I'm going fishing with Nick!' I yelled as I dashed barefoot across the timber floor of our sitting-room and across the cold tiles of the kitchen to the back door. As I yanked it open a damp blast of air hit me.

'Mom! Dad! I'm going fishing with Nick today!' I shouted to the group of horses and riders that had gathered outside the nearby stable. My pyjamas bottoms had ridden halfway up my lower legs, exposing my knobby ankles to the chilling air. Perched like a crane, shifting nervously from one foot to the other, I waited for some sort of reply.

'Sam Fox, do you mind waiting until we get inside?' Mom spoke with lilt in her voice as she lifted a well-worn leather saddle off her big grey mare. She was dressed in a green anorak, corduroy jeans, a black riding-cap and rubber riding-boots.

'I'm half-frozen with the cold. I need a cup of tea before I make any plans.' She smiled at me as she spoke. 'But I do know one thing. You won't be going anywhere except your room if I catch you without your slippers on!'

Mom loved her morning rides with Dad and Clare. The three of them were horse-mad. Mom had a great big Irish draught mare named River Run, Dad a lively chestnut gelding called Casey, and Clare her prize-winning pony, Timber Twig, nicknamed Piggy because of his total obsession with food. The three of them would set off on horseback at the first light of day, rain or shine, to check Dad's cows and horses. They often jumped the single stone walls separating the fields. Clare would go out even on a school day. I honestly didn't see what the big deal was with horses and ponies. I can ride but I just can't be bothered. Fishing is what I like.

'Better go and look for those slippers before

Mom comes in,' I thought. They were probably upstairs under my bed.

'Sam! Breakfast,' Mom called up the back stairs a few minutes later.

I stopped flipping through an old Christmas toy catalogue I had found during my search for my slippers, and resumed rooting things from under my bed. This time I pulled out a dusty, squashed-up athletic bag. When I opened it, I found a forgotten pair of clean sports socks. They'd do! I pulled them on and headed back down to the kitchen.

'Mom, can I phone Nick now?' I asked, executing a human bicycle skid across the tiled floor.

Mom turned from the Aga range where she was frying eggs and sausages, looked down at my covered feet, sighed, and turned back to the range again. I decided to appeal to Dad.

'Dad, can I phone Nick, please?' I begged.

Dad, in a plaid workshirt and faded jeans, was standing next to the kitchen sink, listening to the 9 o'clock news. He stood motionless, his eyes fixed on the small black radio which was broadcasting the news of the day. I knew he was waiting for the weather, the most important item for him.

'Sh!' was his only response. His brow was

lined with concentration and also by constant exposure to rain and sun.

I decided to keep quiet for the moment and slowly lowered myself into one of the straight-back kitchen chairs. Clare was already at the table, studying the horse section from the *Farmer's Journal*. She's a year older than me, tall and skinny with brown hair she always has tied back. She can be a real pain so I gave her plaited pigtail a tweak just to annoy her.

'Ouch! You brat,' she hissed. 'Mom, tell Sam to quit it.'

'Stop, the pair of you.' Mom spoke sharply. 'Breakfast is ready. Now, Sam, what did you want to tell me?' She carried over a large platter of fried sausages and eggs and placed them in the centre of the table.

Around the platter were plates of sliced brown soda bread and hot buttered scones. My stomach growled in anticipation of the glorious meal it would soon receive.

'Mom, I already told you about it yesterday,' I said, exasperated. Stuffing a sausage into my mouth, I continued, 'John Moran is going to some all-day meeting in Galway today...'

'Not with your mouth full,' Mom cut in before turning to Dad. 'Tom, your breakfast is getting cold. Bring over that pot of tea.'

Dad responded by giving a slight grunt and clicked off the radio.

'Go on, Sam. We're all listening.' Mom sounded distracted as she poured out four mugs of tea. Dad sat down and started to eat.

'It's all planned. John has to go to a meeting at some hotel near the sea. There's a fishing lake nearby. John said Nick and I could go over with him, fish for the day, and come back with him in the evening. I've got the worms dug and everything. Can I go?'

John Moran was our local vet as well as a good friend of Mom and Dad's. He often stopped by on his rounds for a cup of tea and a chat about the latest racing results or the likelihood of a local horse running well at the next race-meeting.

Nick was John Moran's nephew. He lived in Meath but came down to stay with his uncle and aunt during all the school breaks. He was dead keen on becoming a vet and wanted all the experience he could get. He had come to Galway for a Halloween break and had two days left before heading home.

'What do you think, Tom?' Mom asked.

Dad looked a bit concerned. 'We don't know the first thing about this lake, plus they might be a bit of a nuisance to John.'

'But, Mom, it was John's idea in the first place,' I argued. 'He was the one to tell us about the lake. He said he was told it was full of brown trout and pike.'

'I don't rightly know,' Dad answered, buttering another slice of brown bread. 'Aren't you a bit young to be jaunting off for a day? When I was your age I'd be up at dawn foddering the cattle and doing odd jobs. Why don't you stay at home and give me a hand? This weather is darn peculiar. It's so dead and heavy for this time of year.'

'But, Dad...' My voice cracked with emotion and my eyes filled with tears. 'You promised to take me fishing all summer and you never did. This will be my last chance till next summer to try out my new fishing-rod.'

'I don't know, Sam...' Mom began but was cut short by the ring of the phone.

'I'll get it.' I jumped to my feet and raced to the front hall to answer it.

'Dad! It's Nick!' I shouted 'He wants to speak to you.' I handed the phone to him and hovered nearby, hoping to pick up bits of the conversation.

'Of course, I trust you,' Dad was saying. 'It's just that bit far away. Is John there?'

I wandered back into the sitting-room

where Mom was poking at the freshly lit turf in the high arched stone fireplace, making small flickers of flame dance between the coal-black sods. It seemed like hours before Dad hung up and joined us.

'Can I?' I asked hesitantly, afraid of what the answer might be.

'I said he could go,' Dad said to Mom. 'I must be daft.'

'Yes! Yes! Yes!' I shouted, punching the air with my fist. 'You're the best, Mom and Dad. When are they collecting me?'

'John said he'd be here in twenty minutes. He needs to be at the Connemara Coast Hotel at ten. He said to wear warm clothes.'

'I'd better make them a packed lunch,' Mom said, getting to her feet. 'Don't worry, Tom, they'll be fine. Nick is almost fifteen and very responsible. He's been a member of the Scouts for years. Look at the way he helped Clare last summer with Piggy. She would never have won the All-Ireland Pony Championship without him.'

'I suppose you're right.' Dad was trying to sound positive. 'Better go and change.'

He added, 'What could happen anyway?'

2 Connemara Bound

'How many fish do you think we'll catch?' I asked Nick, feeling both restless and excited. We were sitting in the back seat of John Moran's Volvo station wagon less than an hour later, on our way to Galway.

'It all depends,' Nick replied, his eyes glued to an illustrated page in a small paperback book he held on his lap. 'There's been an awful lot of rain lately. I think that's good for fishing or is that just in the spring?'

He was talking more to himself than to me. Long brown hair that hung over his ears and eyes and a heavy quilted shirt failed to disguise his bony face and body. No wonder he never wore shorts in the summer; he would have looked like a walking skeleton.

'Listen to this.' Nick raised his voice so that he could be heard by his uncle in the front seat. 'A golden eagle has the sharpest eyesight in the world. It can spot a rabbit from more than half a mile away.'

'I doubt if you'll find any eagles in the bog,' said John. 'But keep an eye out for the curlew. And you might catch a glimpse of snipe or grouse. Skylarks, too. And maybe water-hens on the lake … But of course you'll be too busy fish-spotting.'

He laughed as he swung the car sharply through a wide stone-wall entrance and over to the far side of the car park. 'The Connemara Coast Hotel, at your service.'

'Wow!' I exclaimed, craning my neck to get a good look at the hotel. 'Nick, will you look at all the windows?'

'Note where I'm parking,' said John as we came to a halt, 'so we'll have no trouble finding each other later on. Now let's get your gear unpacked and head up to the hotel.'

He glanced at his watch before opening the back door of the Volvo. Nick and I had the fishing-rods, tackle box, packed lunch, and plastic container of worms on the ground in a matter of seconds. Nick put the lunch inside the rucksack he carried slung over his shoulder and handed me the box of worms.

'You carry these and the tackle box,' he instructed. 'I'll take the rods. You're so giddy I'd be afraid you'd spear one of the hotel guests.'

He smiled and gave me a playful poke in the back with the end of one of the rods.

'We'll ask inside which is the best way to the

lake,' John said, adding, 'We'd better hurry. My meeting started ten minutes ago.'

Nick stretched out his long legs and strode after his uncle; I had to run in order to keep up with them. It was a perfect day; blue skies and just enough wind to make the Irish flag flap on top of the flagpole outside the hotel.

'Here's a leaflet that will show them the route,' the young man behind the reception desk was explaining to John when we rejoined him after leaving our fishing gear under a table in the hotel hallway. 'Tell them to follow walk number 3. When they pass the two-storey house they should turn left and follow the tarred road for about a mile. They'll pass a camp of travellers on the right, just before they get to the lake.'

'Is it difficult to get to the lake from the tarred road?' Nick asked, studying a map of the walking route inside the leaflet.

'No problem,' he replied. 'There's a gravel road down to it. People fish and picnic there all the time.'

'How long will it take us to walk there?' Nick continued as I took a look at the map.

'Twenty minutes or so. It's a pretty walk, bog on one side, rough pasture land on the other. And you've got a good day for it.'

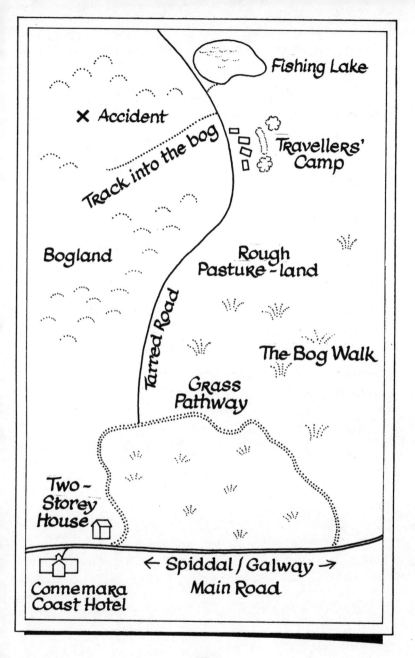

'Thanks,' Nick said. 'Can I have the map?'

'Sure, it's on the house.'

'Are you two all set?' asked John impatiently. 'I'd better scoot off to my meeting. We'll meet back at the car at four. Mind young Sam.'

'Will do, Uncle John,' said Nick cheerfully. 'Who knows, we might have fish for your tea.' He gave me a soft punch in the arm.

'For sure,' I answered with a big grin.

John turned and walked quickly towards a sign pointing to the conference rooms. He turned and waved before he vanished through a door. Nick and I headed for the hall to retrieve our fishing gear.

'This will be great,' said Nick waving the leaflet. 'I'll even get a chance to use my map-reading skills from Scouts.'

3 Ghost Stories

'Here's the two-storey house,' Nick said as we passed an old derelict building with boarded-up windows and padlocks on both the front and back doors. The surrounding yard was full of rusty barrels and broken bits of farm machinery half-hidden by the tall grass.

'What do you think happened to the people living there?' I asked, lowering my voice in case I might be heard.

'They've probably moved into town or something,' Nick replied. 'Come on, keep going or we'll never get to the lake.'

I continued to look back at the old house as I took small half-steps forward.

'Look, here's the tarred road,' Nick said, studying the hotel leaflet. 'At least we're on the right track.' He slid the map back into one of the rucksack's side pockets.

'Nick, do you think that house could be haunted?' I asked hesitantly. We were now walking along the tarred road that would take us to the lake.

'Why would it?' Nick laughed. 'You've been watching too many Casper cartoons.'

The road neatly divided the bogland from the rough pasture land, the browns and yellows of the dying heather and bog grasses contrasting sharply with the greens and greys of the stony pasture land. It was so peaceful. Not a sign of a house or a shed ahead; just a few scattered sheep dotted here and there.

'Nick, do you believe in ghosts?' I asked, still thinking about that lonely house.

Nick studied me for a moment as if trying to figure out if I were joking and then answered me slowly. 'Look, Sam,' he began, 'I don't believe in ghosts but some people do. There are these Irish legends about spirits and fairies. The old people talk about them but I don't know…'

'What kind of legends?' I interrupted.

'Oh, about the banshee and stuff.' Nick sounded bored.

'The what?'

'The banshee, an old fairy woman who comes out at night when a death is about to happen. She's a small wrinkled woman with long white hair that she's always combing. She stands outside the dying person's window and makes a horrible wailing cry, like some trapped hare or half-crazed cat. And if you hear her cry, you will die soon after.

'And then there's this Irish poem we had to learn off in school. It's all about footsteps in the night. Footsteps you hear but there's no one there. It's called *Na Coisithe* by someone called Gogan.

> 'I gcoim na hoíche,
> No coisithe ag siúl.
> Airim iad, ní fheicim iad,
> Ní fios cá mbíonn a gcuaird.

'What it means in English is:

> 'In the middle of the night I hear them,
> The walkers walking.
> I feel them, I don't see them,
> I don't know where they are going.

'It's suppose to scare you but it's all a bit of a cod.' Nick laughed and started whistling some pop tune. He lengthened his stride, ghosts forgotten. As I ran to keep up with him, I couldn't help wondering about the banshee and those footsteps in the night. A shiver ran through me. I was glad it was a bright sunshiny day.

Nick and I walked on silently, the only sound the soft tread of our runners on the gravel and the rhythmic sway of Nick's canvas rucksack on his back.

The peace was rudely broken minutes later by the shrill alarm of my digital watch. I jumped and almost tripped over my feet.

'What's wrong?' Nick chuckled. 'Banshees on your trail?' He gave me a dig. 'You jumped a mile.'

'Can we eat, I'm starving?' I asked, hoping to change the subject. I didn't want Nick to think I was a banshee freak. I remembered the brown-loaf sandwiches Mom always packed, full of ham, cheese and tomato. Also the bags of crisps, satsumas and the chocolate snack bars Clare and I always tucked in as extras.

'Hang in there, pardner,' Nick jested. 'We're almost at base. We'll have our lunch once we get to the lake.'

'But I'm dying of thirst,' I complained. 'Just a drink?'

'You sound like…' He stopped abruptly. 'Look, there's the travellers' camp the man at the hotel told us about. The lake is just beyond it. We're practically there.' He increased his pace once more.

Just as the road took a sharp turn to the right four small white trailers came into view. Two Hiace vans were parked alongside them, one hitched to an open-top horse-box. I could smell burning timber before I saw the thin curl of smoke rising up between the trailers.

A heap of rusty scrap metal and discarded batteries were piled at one end of the camp while a few dullish-brown bales of hay were stacked under an old farm cart at the other end. Along the back of the camp, a line of washed clothes draped the thick roadside hedge. We hurried on in anticipation of our day's fishing.

'Grrr…'

Nick and I froze where we were.

We both looked at each other.

The next moment two masses of bone and fur hurled themselves at us, snarling, teeth

bared and eyes glazed.

I screamed and dived behind Nick who pushed me towards the bank on the far side of the road. I closed my eyes and waited for the clench, the rip, and the tear of teeth. But it didn't come. The growling and snarling continued but not the attack.

When I finally got the courage to look I saw that both dogs, two roany-black greyhounds, all bone and muscle, were struggling to get free of their tethered twines. Why didn't the owners come out and call them off?

'Come on, Sam, let's get out of here,' Nick said, backing away. 'I don't trust that baling twine they're tied with.' He grabbed my arm and pushed me forward on down the road. My legs felt like jelly.

'I was sure we were goners. Did you see their teeth?' I rattled on, still visibly shaken from the fright. 'I bet they're fighting dogs the way they went for us. Why didn't someone come out and stop them?'

'I don't know.' Nick sounded relieved as we put some distance between them and us. 'Let's try to forget it and concentrate on catching some fish. There's the lake; I'll race you to the gravel road.'

4 Brown Trout

The lake was small and full of weeds, the water grey and murky with bits of brown slime floating on the top. A flock of mallards rose out of the water as we approached the edge. A grey heron flapped its arched wings before awkwardly propelling itself into flight, its harsh call an alarm at intrusion.

'Let's head for those rocks,' Nick suggested. 'They'll be dry and warm from the sun. We can have our lunch once we get our lines into the water.'

I followed him along the edge of the lake. Pale, ashy-coloured reeds grew thickly against a backdrop of spindly saplings, their greeny-brown branches now leafless.

We came to a group of rocks that formed a sort of stepping-stone path into the deeper water; a mini giant's causeway into the centre.

'Step where I step,' Nick warned, 'and don't slip. That water has to be cold.'

We managed to find one large flat rock, big enough to let us sit comfortably with all our gear. As Nick opened up my tackle box and sorted through the various hooks and floats, I was still thinking of the vicious dogs. What kind of people owned them? Travellers? I didn't know any, apart from the few who would pull into the yard looking for Dad, trying to sell him farm gates or plastic barrels.

'Here's your line. Watch the hook, whatever else you do!' Nick warned. 'Do you know how to work the release on the reel?'

'Course, I do,' I answered confidently but I waited for him to bait his own hook with one of the slimy earthworms and release enough line to let the float bob freely on the water's surface. I tried to do the same and managed, with a little help, to get my line in on the other side of the rock.

'That's that. Now we wait,' said Nick cheerfully. 'How about some lunch? You hold the rods and I'll unpack the grub.'

I was thrilled to be put in charge of two lines. My chances of a catch were doubled.

Nick divided up the lunch evenly, putting my share on the lid of the plastic sandwich container. He put his share in the container. We dug in, one-handed, leaving the other free to manage the fishing-rod. While stuffing a sandwich into my mouth I looked up overhead. Large billowy clouds filled a grey-blue sky.

'Heaven,' I thought to myself. 'This has got to be heaven.'

'Nick, how come you spend all your holidays in Athenry?' I asked curiously after a few minutes of silence. 'Don't you ever want to go somewhere else?'

'Naw, I like it here,' he replied. 'Mom and Dad and my two younger sisters go to a different holiday spot every year. They always want me to go with them but I won't. I tried going to the south of Spain with them a couple of summers ago but I hated it. I got sunburned and was bored out of my mind.

'I love coming here. And I'm learning a lot as well. I got to give the big Newfoundland a distemper and parvo vaccination last night. Uncle John was there of course to help me hold the dog and stuff. But I did it. It was cool. I gave the injection myself.'

'Hey, look at my float, Nick,' I cried. 'I think I've got a fish. Will I reel it in? Is this right? No, I can do it. Let me, Nick! Wow! Look at that. Is it a trout? It's massive. This is great!'

With Nick's patient guidance and my grim determination we managed to land the trout. I cringed as I watched Nick extract the hook from the trout's mouth and then, to my horror, saw him hit the fish with a heavy stone.

'Why did you do that?' I cried out indignantly. 'The poor fish.'

'I had to kill it fast,' said Nick. 'Did you want it to suffer?'

I felt a knot form in my stomach. Somehow fishing had lost a bit of its appeal.

Nick helped me rebait my hook and we settled down to wait for the second one. The sun had gone but as there was no wind we didn't feel the cold.

'Weather's changing,' said Nick, looking upwards. 'I'd say there's a mist setting in.'

I looked up at the sky and noticed that the puffy clouds and blue-grey sky had become a solid sheet of grey.

'We'd better keep an eye on it.' Nick sounded serious. I said nothing but concentrated on my float, trying to will it to sink below the surface.

'You don't like animals?' Nick asked after a bit. I watched as he shifted his position and stretched out his long legs.

'Oh, I do. I love our sheep-dog, Rex, and Jack Russell, Tiny,' I replied defensively. 'It's just horses and ponies I could do without.'

'It's a pity. Your mom and dad and Clare have great fun riding. Why don't you try it?'

'I know how to ride, I just don't like it,' I answered sullenly, catching a small stone in my free hand and flinging it out across the still lake water.

'Hey, it's okay, Sam,' Nick said gently, 'I didn't mean to upset you. Did something happen to you? You can tell me if you want.'

'Okay, if you must know,' I said slowly, remembering the anger. 'When I was six or seven I went out alone to see a mare and foal that Dad had brought in from the field and put into one of the stables. He had said that the foal looked weak and wanted John to check him. I wanted to see him so, without telling anyone, I let myself into the mare's stable. I knew I shouldn't be there. Dad is always telling us that mares with foals are not to be trusted. Well, I didn't mind his warning this one time. I wanted so much to rub the little foal's head and neck.'

'What happened?'

'I went into the stable and saw the foal lying in the far corner. The mare was eating hay. I walked past her and knelt down beside the foal to rub him. The next thing I remember is feeling my head knocked against the back wall. I glanced behind me and saw the mare, ears flattened, eyes rolling, her body ready to strike out at me again. Dizzy and sore as I was, I managed to climb out through the back window before getting sick all over the place.

'I remember that I crept up the back stairs that night and went to bed. When Mom came up, I told her I had a stomach-ache.'

'And they never found out?' Nick asked, amazed.

'Never,' I answered. 'The next day they wanted to take me to the doctor because I was still feeling sick. But I lied and said that I was feeling better.'

'You probably had a concussion,' said Nick. 'You should have gone and seen someone.'

'Anyway, to this day I won't go near a horse

or pony,' I confided. 'I don't trust them.'

'I don't blame you... Hey, I've got a bite.'

We landed Nick's fish, two inches shorter than mine. The talk drifted to school and hurling. I got another trout and Nick got one but he let it get away. It was his own fault; he wasn't paying attention. I noticed he kept looking up at the sky.

Shortly after, he said to me abruptly, 'Sam, I think we should call it a day.'

'Why?' I asked looking at my watch. 'It's only one o'clock. We still have hours to fish.'

'It's not the time, it's the weather I'm worried about.' he replied, 'I think a mist is beginning to fall. I don't fancy walking back down that tarred road in a fog. If a car were to pass, we'd be knocked flat.'

'Aw, c'mon, Nick,' I begged. 'Don't be a spoil-sport. Can't we stay until we catch one more fish?'

'No way, it's pumpkin hour for us,' he said, starting to reel in his line. 'Get your line in and gear packed. We'll do it again, I promise.'

We retraced our steps back over the rocks and along the edge of the lake. It was much harder this time because of the falling mist. Everything around us seemed to have gone quiet; the stillness was eerie.

I checked my watch as we started back down the tarred road. It was nearly half-past one. I carried our three small trout in a blue plastic shopping bag, along with my tackle box and plastic worm container. Nick still insisted on carrying the fishing-rods. He can be a bit of a pain at times.

'Nick, can you see the trailers?' I asked worriedly. My heart was already racing at the thought of having to pass the dogs again.

'I can't see that far in this mist,' Nick said. 'They should be just around the next bend. It's getting so hard to see.'

He began whistling that same pop tune he had been whistling all day. I was only thinking of the dogs and getting home. Maybe John would buy us a coke at the hotel.

'What was that?'

Nick suddenly stopped and turned toward the bog side of the road.

'What?' I asked, scuffing my runners against some loose gravel in the road.

'Listen,' said Nick. 'Is that someone calling?'

'It's probably a bird,' I said, still thinking of the dogs. 'Let's go. I want to get back.'

'No, Sam,' said Nick. 'It's someone. They're calling for help. I can't see with all the mist but there's someone out there somewhere.'

'Nick,' I pleaded, 'John would want us to get back to the hotel with the mist and all.'

I was desperate. The last thing I wanted to do was to hang around a bog with mist coming down.

'I hear it again,' said Nick. 'We've got to go and see what's wrong.'

Fear and panic swept through me. The thought of going in search of someone or something terrified me.

'Please, Nick,' I cried. 'Let's go back.'

'No. It's the scout's promise to help. We must go!' He recited softly:

'On my honour I promise
That I will do my best,
To do my duty to God and
To my country,
To help other people and
To keep the Scout Law.'

He was already heading down a rough track that led into the bog.

5 The Promise

The bog road, if you could call it that, led us away from the tarred road deep into the bog, now covered with a smoky veil of mist.

Nick did his best to pick his way around the muddy spots and deep puddles on the uneven surface but it was hopeless; our runners were sopping wet in minutes.

Every so often he would cup his hands around his mouth and shout, 'Hello out there!'

He squinted his eyes as if straining to see even the smallest movement. I stared too but apart from the withered sedge at my feet everything had melted away. Occasionally, when the mist parted I could make out the gaping holes where turf had been carved out. There was no sight or sound of anyone or anything.

'Nick, my feet are soaked,' I complained, tugging on his sleeve. 'There's nobody there. Let's go back. I want to get out of this creepy place.' A shiver of cold passed through me.

'Is anybody out there?' Nick shouted again, this time in a slightly different direction. My runners sank into another soft spot on the track. We both stood still and listened.

'What was that?' Nick whispered. 'Sam, did you hear that?'

I desperately wanted to say no and head back to the hotel but I couldn't lie. I *had* heard a low moaning sound.

'Maybe it's a cow or something,' I said.

The thought of finding someone or something hurt or suffering terrified me. Only last year our sheep-dog pup was run over by a car. The sound of his last few gasping breaths and sight of the bright drops of blood falling from his mouth on to the ground sickened me. Then he died in Dad's arms.

'Hello, out there,' Nick called again, this time in the direction he thought the sound was coming from. 'We're coming to help you. Where are you?'

'Nick, I'm scared,' I whimpered. 'Please let's go back. We can get help at the hotel. John will know what to do.' I grabbed his shirt-tail and tried to drag him back toward the tarred road.

'Sam, stop,' Nick said sharply, shoving me so hard I staggered and almost fell. 'Don't start acting the baby. There may be someone hurt out there. We must see if we can help.'

He started walking slowly down the track. I trailed behind. We passed two piles of turf heaped on the edge of the track.

Nick stopped and yelled again. 'We're here. Where are you?'

A low groan came from almost beside us. Between the mist that lurked in the hollows and the long reedy grass that grew over everything, it was hard to see more than a few yards.

Nick and I both knew about the dangers of a bog. Since we were toddlers, parents and friends had always warned us to be careful where we stepped. The side of a turf bank could give way, a hastily made kesh or bridge could collapse, and a swallow-hole could pull you under like quicksand. That was more frightening than anything.

'Sam, the noise is coming from that drain.' Nick's voice sounded hoarse. 'We've got to leave the track and make our way across. Hold my hand in case you fall.'

I was going to beg him to go back for John but the urgent note in his voice silenced me.

'What about our fishing gear?' I asked instead.

'We'll leave it back beside one of those piles of turf. We can get it again on our way back.'

'If we ever get back,' I said under my breath.

We left our gear and made our way slowly

off the track and on to the spongy bed of grass and moss that covered the bogland. Nick grasped my hand and hunched over so that he could use his free hand to feel for weak spots. The air was cold and damp on my face but my back felt hot and clammy.

'We're almost there!' Nick chanted in a whispery voice. 'Hold on. We're coming.'

The groaning now turned to grunting; and there was a new sound, as if someone or something was thrashing about.

With Nick leading me, and taking small cautious steps, we made it across a grassy section to an open drain. Nick fell to his hands and knees and looked in. I did the same. Nothing!

'Can you hear me?' Nick called out again. A scrambling sound came from the drain above and beyond us.

'Help me! Dear God, the pain.' The voice drifted back to a low groan.

Nick, holding my hand, turned and started to move up along the bank in the direction of the voice. I was trembling inside. I could still only see the grassy bank in front of us as we kept creeping forward.

'Here, help me, I'm here.' The voice was now only a few yards away. Then we saw a cart on its side in the drain, barely supported by collapsed planks. One iron-rimmed wheel was suspended in air.

It made no sense to me. Where was the voice coming from?

'Where's the man?' I asked.

Nick was the first to see him. An old man, his face deathly white, was underneath the second wheel. Halfway down the side of the drain, a small pony, still in harness, was caught between the shafts. His eyes were rolling and he was making weak whimpering sounds.

'What happened?' Nick asked as he tried to reach the man by sliding down the drain. There was a sudden scramble and thrashing. The upturned cart teetered.

'Oh, God…stop…the pain,' the old man cried out. 'Whoa, ladeen… whoa.' Nick edged his way back to me.

The struggling stopped. Nick stood still. I had never moved.

'Mister,' Nick whispered. 'What should we do?'

'It's me leg. 'Tis caught beneath the wheel.' He sounded weak. 'I can't stick the pain much longer.'

'We'll try to right the cart,' Nick said softly to me, looking at the broken planks around the

cart. 'He must have been making his way across when the kesh collapsed, pitching the pony and cart into the drain. The weight of the loaded cart was too much for the rotten boards to hold.'

'But how did the man get caught under the wheel?' I asked, also in a whisper.

'I don't know,' said Nick. 'But I do know that we've got to get him out – and fast. He could be bleeding to death, and sitting in the wet drain could kill him just as fast.' His voice had become hoarse with urgency.

'How will we get him out,' I asked.

'We've got to try to tip the cart up,' said Nick. 'Grab hold of the wheel and when I

count three, pull as hard as you can. One…
two… three….'

We tugged with all our might but the heavy
cart only shifted slightly with our effort.
Again, the pony tried to rise and free itself
from the upturned cart.

'Stop, sweet Jesus, for God's sake, stop him,'
the trapped man cried out as the cart moved
on his leg.

'Sam, we've got to try again. We've *got* to
get the cart up.' Nick sounded panicky this
time. 'One, two, three… pull!'

We pulled and pulled until I fell over. The
cart only rocked a bit more. Again, the pony
flung itself forward in fright.

'Stop, stop.' The old man's voice was even
fainter. 'Leave me be, 'tis better this way.'

'Nick, what are we going to do?'

One of Nick's hands still gripped the spokes
of the upturned wheel.

'I don't know, Sam. I don't know,' he
whispered. 'We've got to get him out. He'll die
from the cold. He's hurt. We've got to help
him.'

'Why don't we go back to the hotel and get
John?' I asked. 'He'll know what to do.' The
old man continued to moan softly.

'It will take too long,' Nick said. 'He may be

seriously hurt. His voice sounds very weak. The first thing is to get this cart off him. But we can't do it alone. We've got to get help. Either you or I will have to go for help.'

'But where? You said the hotel was too far away?'

'The travellers, they're nearby. They'll help us... Sam, you go. I'll stay here with the old man. At least I can get the turf out of the cart.'

'Why can't we both go?' I tried to keep the panic out of my voice. I was petrified at the thought of having to face those dogs alone. What if they broke free and attacked me?

'Nick, I can't go,' I cried. 'Please come with me.' I knew Nick must think I was a coward but I didn't care.

'You know I can't, Sam. I can't leave an injured man alone... You've got to go, and go now. Every second counts.'

I turned and headed slowly up along the bank of the drain. All I could think of was how this day I had so looked forward to so much had suddenly turned into a day of gloom.

And it wasn't over yet.

6 The Camp

I looked down at my digital watch. Two-thirty. Only an hour had passed since we had left the lake and started back along the tarred road to the hotel. It seemed like years.

Why, oh why, had I wanted to go fishing? Why did we have to hear that cry in the bog? Why did I have to go back to the travellers' camp and face the dogs alone?

Now they were all counting on me. Nick, the old man, that half-cracked pony. ME! The dope of the family as Clare used to call me. I wondered if I should go back to the hotel and get John. No joy here; I'd still have to pass the camp and the dreaded dogs.

My mumbling and muttering occupied me so much that I didn't realise how fast and how far I had walked until I heard the first menacing growl. I snapped to my senses. I was just approaching the first trailer of the camp. To my relief, I saw that the two snarling dogs were tied under a trailer at the back. I could ask for help without going near them. I also noticed that both Hiace vans were gone .

There was no one in sight.

'Hello,' I called shyly after tapping on the door of the first trailer. 'Anybody there? We need help.'

I waited for a reply. Nothing but the constant growling and snapping of the dogs.

I turned and walked cautiously behind the second and third trailers. The fire of sticks still smouldered, and the ground was littered with plastic containers and pieces of scrap. Against the council fence, where clothes were draped, lay a basket of wet washing. Someone *had* to be inside. I walked quickly around to the front of the second trailer and banged at the door.

'Hello,' I shouted. 'I know there's someone in there. A man's hurt.' No reply.

I ran to the third trailer and banged on the door. The door of the first trailer opened.

'Who's hurt?' A young woman with two small boys clinging to her tight-fitting jeans looked out. 'Is he from around here?'

I stared at her for a moment. She had brassy blonde hair pulled tightly back with a bright blue head-band. She wore big gold hoop earrings and had two gold chains around her neck. The boys, both with close-cropped hair, pressed against her. Her two bare arms and light tee-shirt made me shiver.

'I don't know his name. All I know is he's

caught under his cart in the bog and we can't lift it off him. We need help. Please, please, come,' I begged. Tears were trickling down my cheeks.

She shrugged. 'There's no one here. I can't leave the young 'uns. Where are ye from? Not from around here.'

'No,' I said shortly. Then remembering Mom ('Always be polite'), I appealed again. 'How soon will they be back, Ma'am?'

'The men have gone to Galway with the foal. They won't be back for hours.'

Looking at my anguished face, she seemed to relent. 'Take a bit of rope from the ole cart, if you like. Mind yerself, weather's turned bad.' She looked up at the sky before pushing her boys inside and closing the door.

Silence, except for the barking dogs.

'On my own again,' I thought. 'I'd better go back and tell Nick. I'll take the rope as well: we might be able to pull the cart over with it.'

I took the length of rope from the flat cart. Three dead hares were hanging there, their back legs tied to the shafts of the cart. I felt sick at the sight of them and walked on quickly, my eyes fixed on the ground.

The mist was heavier than before but I was able to follow our footprints on the muddy bog track. I hesitated at the two piles of stacked turf, wondering whether I should bring any of our fishing gear. I decided to take everything except our rods. Maybe the old man would want a drink of orange.

I turned off the track and headed for the drain, uncertain if I was in the right place. Then I saw Nick. I dropped everything but the rope on the ground.

'Nick,' I panted, 'there's no one at the camp except a woman and her two small boys. The others had gone to Galway with a foal.'

'Were both vans gone?' Nick probed.

'Yea,' I said. 'The woman said they'd be

gone for hours. I did my best, Nick, honest.' I felt I had failed him. Another wave of tears trickled down my face.

'It's okay, Sam. You did your best,' Nick said, putting his arm around me. 'Maybe the rope will work. At least I got the cart unloaded.'

'How's the old man?' I asked.

'Weaker, I'd say. He's either bleeding or beginning to get hypothermia. He must have been in that wet drain for hours.' He started to lace the rope through the raised wheel of the cart.

'Have you talked to him?' I asked as I watched him ready the cart.

'Can't. Every time I raise my voice to speak to him or move toward him in the drain, the pony goes berserk and rocks the cart. The poor man can't stand much more pain.'

'Do you think the pony is hurt,' I asked, looking at it, still harnessed to the cart.

'I don't think so. I looked him over as best I could while you were gone There are no cuts or signs of broken bones... Now, we've each got an end of rope to pull on. We've got to brace ourselves down the side of the drain so that we can get some leverage. I'll show you what to do.' He took my end of the rope and slid half way down the drain.

'Slide down to me,' he instructed. 'I'll show you where to put your feet and pull from.'

I followed him, sliding down on the seat of my pants. I was soaked. Between the hike up and down the bog track and half crawling across the grass banks, every piece of my clothing was either damp or wringing wet. Nick was no better off.

He left me holding an end of the rope and headed to the opposite side of the drain to take up his position. I could hear the old man moaning and the pony making the odd rustling sound. I watched Nick ready himself.

'When I say "Go!" pull with every bit of muscle you have,' he shouted over to me. 'We've got to make it happen. The old man is depending on us. Ready… Steady… Go…'

I pulled like I had never done before. I pulled until my knuckles turned white and the power in my arms gave out. The cart shifted slightly but no further than before. It must have been caught on something. Then, as we released our pull, I waited for the cries of the old man.

'Now what?' I asked, when Nick helped me back up the drain.

'I don't know,' said Nick. He sounded in

despair as he rubbed his rope-burned hands. 'He'll surely die the way he is. And we can't get the cart off him.'

'Let's go back to the hotel and tell John,' I pleaded. 'He'll get help. I'm sure there are lots of men who'll help us.'

'No,' said Nick firmly. 'We can't leave the old man here alone. It's scout law: *Do not leave the casualty alone until help arrives.* You'll have to stay here with him while I go. I'll be faster going back to the hotel.'

'No way, Nick,' I said, panicking again. 'You can't make me do it. Not on my own.' I turned my back and started kicking a few withered ferns.

'Sam, it'll be okay,' Nick said. 'Nothing will happen I promise you. I'll be back before you know it.'

'You're just mad because I didn't get help from the travellers.' I spitted my words at him. 'They weren't there. I told you.'

'Sam, I believe you,' soothed Nick. 'I know they weren't there …But there's another reason why I have to go. This mist is turning into fog and you wouldn't be able to find your way back to the hotel. You'd get lost and I can't risk it.'

'Nick,' I said desperately, 'please don't make

me stay alone with a dying man. I'm afraid. I'm really afraid. I can't do it.' I pulled on his damp shirt.

'Of course you can do it,' Nick encouraged. 'You're tough. It'll only be for a little while. Just talk to him… and sooth the pony.'

He walked over to his rucksack and pulled out the hotel leaflet with the map, then reached in his pocket, got his compass and put it back again.

'Listen, Sam,' he instructed. 'Don't move from here. Stay beside the cart no matter what. Do you understand? I'll be back with help as soon as I can.'

'How long will you be,' I asked, trying to sound strong.

'I might be only twenty minutes,' said Nick. 'I'll check the travellers' camp first to see if anyone has come back. If that fails I'll make my way to the hotel as fast as I can. John's car will drive us back.'

He gave me a dig in the ribs, and walked carefully along the bank of the drain.

I watched him until he disappeared into the thickening mist.

7 Nightmare!

I shivered as I watched Nick disappear into the heavy mist. The air was getting cooler, making my damp clothes feel even more uncomfortable. I looked at my watch again. Three-thirty. John would be expecting us in less than an hour. The thought of him warmed me for a moment. Slumping to the ground, next to my tackle box and leftover picnic lunch, I decided to set my alarm. Nick had promised to be back with the travellers in twenty minutes. I felt I could wait that long, unless I went crazy first listening to the old man's cries. At least the pony was quiet.

If only I could manage to block out the sounds of the old man. Maybe by thinking of something else, like being home on the farm with Mom and Dad and Clare. Or messing with my friends in the apple orchard.

It was no use; I couldn't concentrate. I was up on my feet again, pacing up and down. Twenty to four – that ten minutes seemed like forever. The fog was everywhere around me. A great wall of grey imprisoned me, locked inside with a dying man and his cracked-brain pony. I began to feel nervous. What was there to stop someone sneaking up behind me? I'd never see him until he was on top of me. I saw it happen once in a western on the telly; the poor bloke didn't know what hit him until he felt hands grip his neck and squeeze out his last breath of life.

It could happen and happen here. No one would find me for days in this deserted bog-hole. The old man, my only witness, would also be dead from the cold or his injury. What chance would I have…

'Whee!'

A high-pitched noise pierced the silence.

'What was that?' I whispered, feeling my heart stop and then beat wildly. 'It's got to be the wind.' But I knew it wasn't. I knew full well that nothing had stirred. Why hadn't the pony moved. Surely he must have heard the noise. Or maybe he was dead.

'Whee!' Again it sounded. This time it had almost a human-like tone to it.

'What is it?' I asked myself.

A moment later the answer came like a thunderclap.

'*Whenever death is near*,' Nick had said. It was the banshee coming for the soul of the old man! The idea rocked me so hard that I collapsed to my knees.

'Could it be possible?' I thought. I had tried not to listen to his cries. Now I would have given anything to hear the smallest sound.

'Whee!'

The eerie cry was now followed by other sounds. Something rustling through the bog grass. The clanking of a heavy chain.

My body shook with fear. I thought of the stories Dad told us of sheep being attacked by dogs. The sheep would simply lie down in sheer fright and wait to be killed. Just like me, hunched over terrified, waiting for the jaws of the attacker.

'Whee!' It came again. Again in sequence. The wail…the rustle…the clinking-clanking.

'It's coming closer,' my brain kept telling me. 'That horrible woman is coming closer.'

'Go away,' I tried to shout bravely but my voice was cracked and choked. 'He's not dead, I tell you. The old man is alive and there's help on the way. Go back from wherever you came. He's going to live, I tell you.'

But the sounds just kept coming closer and closer, getting louder and louder. The awful wail, the stealthy rustling, the clinking of metal. I couldn't take it any more. I screamed like I have never screamed before. My throat went raw with the effort.

Then I heard a whinny. The pony in the drain stuggled and the old man cried out with pain as the wheel shifted on his leg.

Would this horrible nightmare never end?

Moments later, my head cradled in my hands and my body stooped on the ground, I peeked between my fingers with a kind of sick curiosity, out into the fog and towards the sound.

There, slowly approaching, was a figure followed by a larger shape. I closed my eyes again and felt warm tears trickle into my cold hands. Should I run? Should I scream for help? What was the point. I had nowhere to go and there was no one to hear me.

I felt my body relax like the innocent sheep waiting for her violent end to come.

8 Red Mick and Mary

'What's wrong with ye?' I heard a blunt voice ask.

I looked up in utter disbelief. A young girl stood there, looking down at me. She had piercing blue eyes and thin yellow-gold hair that fell down past her shoulders. Her upturned nose had a heavy dusting of freckles, and she was dressed in worn corduroys, a denim jacket, and black wellingtons.

It took me a moment to grasp that my banshee was real and alive and staring at me, still waiting for my answer. I slowly climbed to my feet. Behind her, a man loomed out of the mist. He was standing beside the upturned cart, a sturdy piebald pony in working harness beside him. I could hear the piebald softly nickering to the pony trapped between the shafts.

It was now beginning to make sense to me. The rustling had been the feet and hooves as they crossed the bog. The clanking of the chains came from the piebald's harness. But what had made the wailing sound?

'Are ye the lad that's hurt?' the girl asked

quite impatiently. She stood with her two hands on her hips, ignoring my shaken state.

'No,' I said. 'He's trapped under the cart. We heard him from the road, crying out. My friend has gone for help. Are you from the camp on the road? Did you see him?'

If she heard me, she didn't bother to answer, but turned suddenly and walked over to the man. He was roughly dressed. A big, dark, heavy coat, a worn cap pulled over his eyes, thick work boots and baggy trousers covered with stains. His nose, flattened to one side of his unshaven face, gave me the creeps.

They must be from the camp, I thought. Nobody else knew that we were here. But where was Nick? Why hadn't he come back?

'Is that ye, Mr. Broderick?' I heard the traveller call out in a low raspy voice. 'Where are ye caught?' The pony between the shafts immediately panicked at the sound of a new voice and tried to scramble up the drain. The cart jiggled and made the old man cry out.

The traveller took off his heavy coat and with an well-aimed flick tossed it over the head of the frightened pony. It made one more struggle, then yielded to the reassuring comfort of darkness. I watched in amazement.

'Tell me, Mr Broderick, sir,' the man asked

again. 'Tis the wheeleen or the cart?' The hooded pony did not stir.

I heard a feeble whisper from the drain.

'Tis ye, Red Mick. Thank God ye've come...' There was a long pause. 'Tis me foot that's caught between a wedgeen and the wheel. The pain...' The voice faded away.

Did they know each other? Were they relations? Where did the young girl fit in? I stood there looking at them, mouth open.

'Mary,' Red Mick called to the girl who was still standing beside the piebald. I guessed her age to be eight or nine. 'Take a hold of the reins. I'm goin to cut the little horseen free. Then we'll lift the cart.'

Mary grabbed the long rope reins that lay tangled up between the harness of the fallen pony and the shafts of the cart, untwisted them, and brought them forward over the pony's covered head. Without a word, Red Mick took out a small penknife.

First he cut the leather strap that held the wooden hames together on top of the thick collar. They snapped apart, releasing the tension on the harness chains that held the pony between the shafts of the cart. Then he cut through the leather straps on the outside of each shaft. These had held the breeching firmly in place so that the cart could not make contact with the pony. All the time the poor thing lay perfectly still.

'Mary,' he said quietly, 'lift off the coat and give him his head.'

The girl slackened the reins and gently grasped a corner of the coat. With a lifting motion, she raised it off his head, and moved as far away from him as the reins would let her. The pony's ears were flattened and his dark eyes blinked furiously.

'Stay where ye are,' whispered Red Mick. 'I'll bring the mare around.' He slowly walked over to the piebald, grasped her reins, and made a low clucking noise before leading her over to the trapped pony.

'Here's a nice little mare for ye,' he said quietly, letting her sniff the pony's nose and neck. 'Will ye git up for us?' he continued to coax. 'Ye poor horseen. Up ye git from that cold ole drain. Sooner ye're up, sooner we git Mr Broderick free.'

As he spoke he moved the piebald a couple of steps away from the pony. We waited and watched. Several moments later, the pony made a terrible grunting noise as he struggled to get his hind legs under him.

'Ask him, Mary,' Red Mick instructed. Mary

took up the slack in the reins and made the same low clucking noise. The old man's pony, now on his feet and freed from the cart, made a huge lunge and scrambled up out of the drain on to the solid bank.

'Pull him, Mary,' Red Mick yelled. 'Pull him as far as ye can.'

Mary tugged as hard as she could on the reins, stretching out the pony's head and neck. The traveller dropped the reins of the piebald and ran behind the hind end of the pony yelling, 'Yip! Yip! Go on!' until his hindquarters crumpled on to the ground below him. They had managed to pull him several yards away from the upturned cart.

'Leave him be,' said Red Mick to Mary, who was still holding the reins. 'We need to git Mr Broderick out. Let the young lad mind him.'

He turned, walked the mare back to the upset cart and unfastened one of the thick rope reins from her bridle. He fixed the end of the other rein in its place. Mary, meanwhile, looked at me and held out the pony's reins. I was petrified at the thought of looking after the half-crazed pony but was even more afraid of refusing. I hesitantly walked forward and took them. With a sideways step, she darted back to the traveller.

'Stay with the mare,' he said to Mary as he draped the unfastened rein around his neck and headed for the side of the drain.

I watched him as he carefully let himself down the side and made his way over to the injured man. He took the rope rein and tied it to the axle of the wheel that was so painfully trapping his foot.

I had almost forgotten what I was supposed to be doing until I heard a weak grunting sound beside me. I looked down at the prostrate form of the pony. His short strong body, splattered with mud and sweat, lay motionless except for his heaving sides. He lay like a dying animal, too spent from his efforts and injuries to rise. He was jet-black in colour except for a broad white mark starting at his forehead and extending down over his trembling nostrils. His eyes were open and staring, with the whites showing.

'Mary, catch the rope,' Red Mick shouted from the drain, heaving the long rope rein over the width of the upturned cart. 'Back the mare into the cart alongside the drain.'

She did exactly what she was told, guiding the docile mare into place. I continued to watch and listen, never loosening my hold on the reins of the lifeless pony at my feet.

'Tie the end to the trace chains. Be sure it's right.'

Mary drew back the heavy work chain hooked to each side of the hames and collar along the outside of the mare's body until they met a few feet from her tail. She then threaded the rope rein through the two end rings of the chain and knotted it firmly.

'Git up, Gypsy,' she said softly to the mare, slapping her side gently with the shortened reins she still held in her hands. The mare walked forward away from the cart, taking up any slack between her and the far axle. When she felt a pull, she instinctively stopped.

'Whoa, girl,' Mary called. 'Easy now.'

Red Mick moved to the shaft end of the cart to see if Gypsy was in the right position.

'Good, Mary,' he grunted. 'Now take it handy, the planks are red rotten. Tis a miracle Mr Broderick is still alive.'

He moved back to the old man and the taut rope. I could hardly bear to watch.

'Go on, Gypsy.' Mary spoke again to the mare, and gave the same gentle slap with the reins. Gypsy hesitated as she felt the weight of the cart. She then leaned forward, using her powerful back and shoulder muscles, and began to take small steps forward. The cart began to right itself as she continued to pull.

'Quick, Mr Broderick,' I heard Red Mick shout. 'The cart could tip again.' He grabbed the old man around his chest and pulled him to his feet. The screams of agony were terrible. 'Ye'll be right as rain once we git ye up the bank,' he coaxed as he shoved him forcefully to the side of the drain where the pony had been caught.

'Have mercy, please God, have mercy,' Mr Broderick pleaded weakly as he tried to lie down. I could see his face – ghostly white and contorted with pain. His lips were ice-blue.

'Up ye git, Mr Broderick,' Red Mick continued to urge as he pushed him up the side of the bank. 'Ye can't fool me, ye're as tough as old bags.'

I watched in wonder and silent admiration as the traveller pushed and shoved the injured man up on to the bank a few yards away from where I stood, still holding the reins of the collapsed pony. The old man, his face beaded with sweat, lay limp in Red Mick's strong arms.

'I'll put you near the heather. Ye'll be the finest... Mary,' he shouted, 'put me coat over Mr Broderick.' She quickly retrieved the dark coat that had been left on the ground after pulling it off the pony's head and put it gently over the old man, covering his chest and legs. 'Now, make a bit of a pillow for him.' He took off his inside jacket and handed it to her. Then he gestured towards Gypsy. 'Ease her off and untie the rope.'

My eyes moved from the figure of Mr Broderick to Gypsy and the cart, now resting on the damaged bridge. The old man and the small black pony were at last out of the drain. The nightmare was over.

But where was Nick?

9 Stranded

Red Mick looked down at Mr Broderick and frowned. 'I best get a fire started. He'll surely die with the cold and wet from that drain.'

He walked over to some bushes and started breaking branches. I could almost feel the spiky thorns of the furze cut into my own hands. How could he do it without gloves?

He emerged moments later with five or six withered branches that he broke into smaller pieces and put in a pile a few feet away from the old man. Picking up a handful of turf fragments that Nick had thrown out of the cart, he placed them carefully on top of the heap. He took a box of matches out of his trouser pocket, lit one, and set the gorse alight. A spiral of smoke rose straight up in the windless sky before the furze burst into flame under the layer of turf.

'Now, Mr Broderick, sir.' Red Mick knelt down beside the old man whose head was cushioned and slightly propped up. 'I think we'd better get this wellington off your bad foot.'

The old man's face grimaced and he began

to make a new kind of whimpering sound. I could see that the boot on his bad leg was swollen tight, so he must really be hurting. Red Mick took the penknife out of his pocket.

'I'll just give it a little cut to help it off, Mr Broderick.' He talked to him like the doctor had talked to me when he was stitching a gash in my head, kind of humouring him.

'Now just another wee cut near the ankle and ye'll be the grandest.' He carefully held the old man's wellington away from his leg and deftly cut the outside of the boot from the ankle straight upwards. Then he made a cut from the ankle down along the foot. The sides of the rubber boot fell apart.

'Now, Mr Broderick,' Red Mick said, putting his penknife back into his pocket. 'One quick pull and we'll have ye right.' He lifted up the heel of the injured foot and with a fast jerk pulled the boot off the injured leg.

'Owwwwww...' The old man let out a blood-curdling scream. The cry even made the fallen pony raise his head for a moment.

'Ye tramp!' Mr Broderick spitted out the words in a whisper. 'Yer nothing better than a bloody tramp. I hope ye rot in hell.'

I heard a giggle and turned to see Mary laughing into her hands.

'Now, Mr Broderick,' Red Mick said lightly. 'Ye don't mean that. See, yer boot is clean off.'

'Red Mick, I swear when I'm healed, I'll git ye for that.' The voice sounded stronger.

'Yer temper suits ye, Mr Broderick. Ye sound better already.'

I looked over at Mary who was still finding the whole scene comical. I did as well, until I looked back at the old man and saw his foot. With the wellington off all you could see was a round mass the size of a turnip, encased in a bloody black sock. I could also see fresh blood glistening as it seeped through the already soaked sock.

'Mary, will ye gather up a few bits of moss?' Red Mick pulled out his shirt from under his woolly jumper. He reached into his pocket again for his knife and, with a quick slit and a steady pull, I saw him rip his shirt-tail from one end to the other. Mary was back almost as fast with three huge clumps of green moss.

'Good girl. Will ye place it on Mr Broderick's foot once I git his sock off. We need to git the blood stopped.'

I watched again as the traveller eased the blood-soaked sock off the old man's foot. Mr Broderick roared and cursed again but Red Mick never stopped what he was doing. Mary then knelt down and placed a large piece of moss against the bleeding foot – green side to the wound – while Red Mick wrapped his shirt-tail around the foot. I wondered what Nick would think of this 'cure'?

'There ye are, Mr Broderick. Ye'll be good as new.' Red Mick got to his feet and frowned at the fire, which had now gone out.

'The turf is too fresh to light. I must git a bit that's drier or we'll never git Mr Broderick warm. If only he had a hot drink?'

'I have a flask of tea, mister,' I said.

Red Mick turned and stared at me, as if noticing me for the first time. His piercing eyes, half-closed by a squint, studied me closely. I began to regret my offer.

'Ye've a flask?' he asked me. He was not a tall man but strong and stocky, with powerful arms. His worn cap, once checked but now smudged grey, hid his hair, but his grey whiskery chin and deep wrinkles revealed the face of another old man.

'It's with our picnic things over there beside the drain.' I pointed, still holding one hand on the reins. Mary came over to see what was going on. She made it quite clear by her cocky stance and hands on her hips that I was at the bottom of the pecking order.

'Mary, ye and the young lad give Mr Broderick a drink of tea. I'll go back to the reeks and fetch a lock of turf.' He turned and disappeared quickly into the fog which still swirled around us.

'What else ye got?' Mary asked inquisitively. 'Any bars or crisps?'

'Only a few sandwiches,' I stammered.

'Well, git them.' She looked me straight in the eye.

'I can't. What about the pony?' I mumbled. 'I've got to hold him.'

'Ha, ha, ha!' She burst out laughing. 'He ain't goin nowhere by the look of him.'

'What do you mean?' I asked, still gripping the reins.

'He's only fit for the knacker's yard,' she explained. 'Dog food, ye know.'

I looked down at the pony's lifeless form. He was deathly still, except for his steady breathing and shivering. How could she be so cruel?

'Will ye git the tea,' she ordered, grabbing the reins out of my hand and giving me a shove. I got the flask and the two plastic mugs we had used earlier at the lake; also the box of leftover sandwiches.

'There's no sugar. Do you think he'll mind?'

I asked as I knelt down beside the old man who was still moaning.

'What of it,' she replied. 'Give him a cup and I'll take the other. What kind of sandwiches ye got?' Without waiting for an answer she opened the plastic lid and grabbed two of the three remaining ones.

'Here, Mr Broderick,' I said, holding out a half-full cup of milky tea. 'I'll hold it steady so you can drink it.' I held it in front of his lips until he managed to sip it down. I refilled it and held it once more. Meanwhile Mary had poured herself a cup of tea, downed it, and devoured the first ham sandwich. Now she was making quick work of the second.

'Are you a traveller from the camp up the road?' I asked as the old man pushed the cup away, indicating that he had had enough.

'Sort of,' she said but didn't explain. She pointed to the third and last sandwich in the box. 'Don't think he wants that.'

An approaching rustle made me look up. Red Mick was returning, a plastic fertilizer bag filled with turf thrown over his back. He dropped it next to the quenched fire.

'Ye right?' he asked us, before dumping the turf out of the bag and on to the ground.

'We gave him tea,' Mary replied, finishing

off the last sandwich.

'Now, Mr Broderick,' he said confidently, 'Red Mick will build ye a fire!'

I watched as he gathered the thorny withered branches and broke them up as kindling. Then he replaced the turf with the drier bits he had just gathered and draped the plastic fertilizer bag on top before setting the furze alight. This time the smoke did not go straight up but had to curl under the plastic bag. I could see the flames through the white plastic until they burned so hot they melted holes in it. The holes spread, throwing out an intense heat which left drops of burning

plastic on the sods below. Flames roared up through the furze, making a bonfire out of the small pile of turf. Was this how scouts lit a fire?

'Excuse me, mister,' I said to Red Mick who was adding more turf to the already well-caught fire. 'Would you mind taking me as far as the lake road? I have to get back to the hotel. I should have been there at four, and now it's nearly five?' I took off my digital watch and flashed on the light to highlight the time. Mary, who was standing beside me, immediately grabbed it and starting pushing all the buttons. I grabbed it back.

'Ye'll get nowhere tonight, young lad,' Red Mick replied, poking the fire with a piece of broken plank from the kesh. 'The bog ain't safe to cross till the fog lifts.'

'But you crossed it to get the dry turf?' I was now feeling a bit more sure of myself and desperately anxious to get back. John would be wondering where we were unless Nick had already made his way back to the hotel.

'Tis no length to the reeks.'

'When do you think the fog will clear?' I asked worriedly.

'On a windless night like this,' he said, 'might be morning before it starts to clear.'

'You mean we might have to stay here all night?' I asked. 'And what about Mr Broderick? He's got to get to hospital.'

Panic was beginning to grip me again. Where was Nick?

'We need the cart to git him out.' Red Mick went on warming his hands over the fire. 'He'll make the morning, ye can be sure.'

'It's just…' I began.

'Would ye be so mean to leave that small fella behind?' he interrupted, looking over to the pony who was still lying on his side.

I looked as well and thought of the cruel thing Mary had said earlier.

'That's the way of it. It's all Mr Broderick, nothing about the pony – who's just as cold and scared and hurt!'

'Sorry, I'll wait till the pony's fit to travel,' I told him, meaning every word of it.

I looked over to where Mary was sitting up on Gypsy's back while the mare grazed the grassy bank peacefully. 'I'll show *her* what's fit for dog food!'

10 Courage

The turf fire burned brightly against the dreary backdrop of fog and fading daylight. The four of us sat staring into the fire, grateful for its heat. The piebald mare grazed by the side of the drain while the small black pony lay lifeless in the dark shadows.

'Pity we have no grub,' Red Mick said, breaking the silence. He took out an unfiltered cigarette and lit it, before passing it to the old man who accepted it and took a long draw before handing it back. His face had taken on a healthier shade.

'I've got three trout in a plastic bag that we caught today,' I offered, thinking of the three ham sandwiches that the girl had selfishly wolfed down an hour or so earlier. 'But we have no pan to cook them in.'

'Did ye hear that, Mr Broderick?' Red Mick said, giving the old man a playful poke in the arm. 'No frying-pan! Ye remember the days up in Loughwell when we'd set off for an evening's fishing. Remember not wantin' to go home and cookin' them fish then and there over a fire. Nothin' ever tasted so grand.'

Mr Broderick didn't answer but seemed to listen and relax a bit. Maybe he, too, was thinking of the past.

'Could we try and cook the fish?' I asked, feeling my stomach grumble at the mention of food.

'I hate fish.' Mary made a disgusted face. 'Ye'd be daft to eat them.'

'Hush, girl,' Red Mick chided. 'Now... I need a bit of wire. I reckon there'll be some in the dump beside the reeks. I'll go back and see.'

He stood up and began walking away. I scrambled to my feet and followed. I didn't want Mary to hear what I had to say.

'Wait, mister,' I whispered, tugging on the back of his jumper. 'I need to ask you something,' He stopped and turned to me.

'I know this sounds crazy,' I spluttered out. 'It's just that I feel so bad for the pony. Can't you do something for him like you did for the old man? I'm afraid of ponies but I don't want him to die.' My voice choked as tears rolled down my face. I felt stupid but I somehow knew he'd understand.

'Ye poor lad.' Red Mick smiled down at me. 'Ye're worried sick. Tell ye what. I'll find some sort of ole cover for him in the dump. I reckon he's half-killed with the cold.'

'Thanks,' I whispered back as fresh tears welled up in my eyes.

'Git back to the fire and warm yerself,' he said gently.

I watched him go and felt a shiver of cold pass through me as I returned to the fire.

'Now what's wrong with ye?' Mary said sarcastically when I sat down beside her. She must have known I had been crying.

'Nothing's wrong. I just wish I was back on the farm,' I stammered. I was determined not to start crying again or let on about my concern for the pony.

'Don't ye think this is great crack?' she said, poking the fire with the same stick Red Mick had used.

'It's okay but... don't you wish you were home?' I asked.

There was a long pause as if she wasn't going to answer. Then it came.

'I don't have a ma or da,' she said in a low voice, her eyes glued to the ground.

'What do you mean?' I asked. 'You've got to have them.'

'They were killed in a car crash when I was a baby,' she said, still staring at the ground.

'But who minds you?'

'I live with me auntie and granny in a house in Galway. I hate it there.' She sounded angry.

'Why?' I was puzzled. Who was Red Mick?

'Dunno.' she said turning away. It was clear no more information would be forthcoming. I sat back and looked above the bright flames of the fire at the prostrate form of the pony.

'Mr Broderick, what's your pony's name?' I asked, knowing he might not hear me.

'Probably doesn't have a name,' Mary rudely interrupted. 'Me grand-da's mare is called Gypsy. She's a ten-year-old and has had six foals. I got me a lovely two-year-old filly back at the camp.'

So she *was* Red Mick's grand-daughter and they *were* both from the camp.

We didn't have to wait long until we heard the sound of someone coming. It still sounded creepy – even though I knew who it was this time.

He came out of the dense fog like a ghost, carrying a roll of something over his shoulder and a twisted length of wire in one hand. He made his way over to the small pony, unrolled the matting and placed it gently over the back of the frightened animal. The pony struggled a little as he felt the weight settle on his back, then relaxed as he felt its warmth and shelter.

Now the only part of him that was visible was his black head.

'Who's ready for fish?' Red Mick said making his way toward us. 'Lad, get yer fish and, Mary, stoke up the fire.'

He broke off two long thin branches from the furze, then with his penknife he cut off the side shoots, leaving two sticks each about three foot long. I watched him push down the broken end of one stick into the soft peat about a foot from the fire. He did the same thing with the other stick on the opposite side of the burning turf. He took the fish from me and laid the three small trout on the bag. With two swift cuts each, he had their heads off and their bodies split and gutted.

'Lad, do ye have a bit of fresh water to clean them with?' he asked as he lifted the backbone out of each fish.

'Jays, they stink,' Mary remarked, holding her nose.

I dashed back with a bottle of white lemonade. 'Fraid this is all that's left,' I said. He twisted off the cap and rinsed each fish with the liquid.

'Might make them tastier,' he kidded, giving me a wink and laying them back on the plastic bag while he cleaned the blade of his knife on a fresh piece of grass.

'Now, Mr Broderick, sir,' he said to the old man. 'Yer tea will be up in no time.' He picked up the piece of barbed wire and twisted it tightly around the top of one of the sticks in the ground. Then he drew the wire across the top of the fire, secured it to the top of the other stick, and stuck each fish, belly side down, on to one of the barbs. When he was finished he wiped his hands on the grassy bank before sitting down beside Mr Broderick.

'Tis a grand smell,' he exclaimed.

I slipped away, over to the pony, and went slowly up to him. I didn't want to surprise or frighten him. His small head lay on the ground but I could tell he was watching me as I approached. As I got nearer he struggled to lift his head and I could see that the skin around his other eye was torn and swollen from banging it off the muddy ground.

He still wore the bridle that was now caked with grass and mud. The long reins that I had held so tightly were still lying where Mary had thrown them.

'Little pony, I don't know your name,' I whispered, feeling the tears roll down my cheeks and my throat block. 'Please don't die. We'll get help for you too. John Moran is a vet and he'll know what to do. Just, just don't die.'

I sank to my knees and stretched out my hand. I could feel his warm breath as he smelled my fingers. I slowly let my hand drop until my fingers touched his soft pinky-white muzzle. I could feel him cringe at my touch and then relax to the gentle stroking.

'Fish is up,' I heard Red Mick shout. I rose to my feet; I didn't want Miss Bossy Boots to see what I was doing.

'I'll be back,' I promised before making my way back to the fire.

Red Mick looked at me as if to say, 'I understand.'

I watched him untwist the wire from around one of the sticks and bring it around and away from the flaming turf, the trout still held by the barbs. Then he took a small stick that he had pared clean and stuck it into one of the blackened fish. He lifted it off the barbed wire and handed the stick to me.

'First fish to the rightful owner,' he said smiling. I saw he had only a few teeth which should have made him look scary but it didn't. He sort of reminded me of what a small friendly giant should look like.

'Now ye peel off the skin,' he said showing me how to do it with the second fish. 'Mind, it will burn ye,' he warned as he expertly flaked off the charred skin. 'Mary, hold this one for Mr Broderick. We'll let it cool' He took the third fish, stuck it on a stick, and peeled it before I even got mine started. It was still too hot for me to handle.

'Here lad, take mine.' he said, giving me his and taking mine to peel.

'Jays, yer mad to eat those,' Mary piped up as the traveller sat down next to the old man.

'I'll feed him a bit of the cooled one,' Red Mick said taking the fish Mary was holding and handing her the one he held. 'Yer in for a treat.' He pulled off a small morsel and fed it to Mr Broderick.

I blew on my fish before doing the same and popped a small piece into my mouth. It was delicious; hot, sweet, and slightly charred. Mary did not eat; she sat by the fire and continued to poke at the reddened sods of turf.

'How do you know Mr Broderick?' I asked when I has finished my fish and thrown the stick into the fire. I looked at both men trying to puzzle it out.

Red Mick gazed at the old man before he spoke.

'Mr Broderick and I are old friends,' he began. 'I used to help him turn the hay and save the turf long before yer time. He lives up in Loughwell where we used to camp in the old days – I mean before we had caravans and trailers. We used to sleep in tents by the side of the road and git what we needed from the local folk. Mr Broderick always had a fresh can of milk for us each day and a welcome for me and me family. I used to give him a hand whenever I could.'

'But how did you know he was the one caught under the cart?' I asked

'The ole cart,' he chuckled. 'I'd know it from hundreds. Many a day I near killed meself in this bog, cutting turf, footing it, and then throwing it up in that cart. Them were hard times.'

'Did you ever have good times?' I asked.

Mary elbowed me and gave a giggle. 'Yer too young to know.'

'I'm older than you,' I snapped back. 'I was ten last month.'

'Ha, told ye,' she retorted. 'I'll be eleven at Christmas. Told ye. Yer just a baby.'

I stared. I couldn't believe she was older than me.

'Easy, Mary,' Red Mick cut in. 'Ye've too much to say. The lad ain't harmin' no one.' He turned back to me. 'We had good times, Mr Broderick and me. We'd do a bit of hunting and fishing and drink a few pints at Mully Doon's. Those were the days.'

He got up, threw a few more sods of turf on the fire and fixed the heavy coat up around the old man's shoulders.

'I must look at the ole cart,' he said. 'We might be shifting Mr Broderick before long.

Did he know something we didn't? Had he heard something or seen something? And what would happen to the little pony if we did 'shift' soon?

11 The Black Pony

'Whee!' That piercing plaintive cry floated through the still air. My heart began to race.

'Whee!' There it was again. What was it? I looked at my companions. Mary was busy chewing the nail of her baby finger, Mr Broderick had dozed off, Red Mick was off repairing the damaged cart.

'Now what's wrong with ye?' she asked in an annoyed tone. 'Ye'll end up in a mental home, ye will.

'What is it?' I asked.

'Whee!' Again the melancholy wail pierced the eerie stillness.

'Ye're afraid, aren't ye?' she mocked and started to laugh. 'Ye're such a baby. It's only a stupid bird.'

'Are you sure?' I asked.

'What else would it be? A Halloween ghost? Ha… ha…' I waited for a few minutes but she wasn't going to give me an answer.

'What kind of bird?'

'Some weirdo called a curlew.' She twisted a thin strand of hair around her forefinger. 'It's brown with a long curvy beak. Makes that strange noise just before dark.'

'Thanks,' I said reassured, thinking how mist makes everything seem more terrifying.

I got up to stretch my legs and throw a few more sods on the fire and pull the coat up around Mr Broderick's shoulders. His eyes were closed but I could see he was still alive by the heaving of his chest. I returned to my spot next to the fire.

'What class are you in?' I asked, hoping it was a safe subject to talk about. I didn't feel up to being laughed at again.

'Dunno,' she replied, still playing with her hair and staring into the fire.

'What do you mean, that you don't know? 'You're in school, aren't you?'

'Yea, when they make me go.' She spat out the words. 'I hate school. I hate being made to feel different.'

'How do you mean "different"?'

'Them teachers make me sit in the back of the class. All I do is copy this and copy that, colour this and colour that. Then I get blamed for everything. Even if it wasn't me. They hate travellers.'

'Why don't you tell your aunt?' I suggested. 'She could help you.'

'Nah, she's mad at me too.' Mary shrugged

her shoulders. 'Cause I keep runnin' away. Do ye blame me for hatin' the city?'

'I can see you have it rough at school, but why hate Galway. It's a cool place. It's got the cinema, go-karting, Supermac's, the shopping centres. There's so much to do! I wish we lived there.'

'Maybe for ye,' she replied. 'But for me it's borin'. I feel like a cooped-up hen in that council estate. The only thing to do is watch the telly and go to the shop. I'd much rather be here with my grand-da on the open road.'

'Why?' I asked, thinking how small and cramped those trailers must be inside.

'I'm free here, free as a bird.' Her voice lifted and she actually sounded happy. 'There are so many things to do in the country. I can gather sticks for the fire or go fishing in the lake. I can go off with the men to hunt hares or help them break in a young pony. This is where I belong.'

'I kind of know what you mean,' I said slowly. 'We live on a farm and there are always jobs to be done. Bringing in the turf, feeding the dogs, gathering the eggs, sweeping the yard, giving water to the horses and ponies.'

'Ye've ponies.' Her eyes lit up. 'Aren't they the best? Grand-da said I'll be fit to race a pony next summer. Can ye…'

'Mary,' Red Mick called from the cart.

She jumped to her feet and dashed off to help, leaving me alone with Mr Broderick. He seemed peaceful as he dozed. I wondered if he had a family worrying about him. I hoped Nick had made it back to the hotel. Otherwise John would be worried sick. But I was sure he had. Surely that's what scouts were all about.

I wondered what they were doing at home. Probably thought I'd had a great day and was now wolfing toasted sandwiches and tea in the bar at the Connemara Coast instead of sitting, lost in a bog, on damp ground, soaked to the skin, mist all around me. Boy, what I'd have given to be in my warm pyjamas and wrapped in my quilt in the big armchair.

A pawing sound broke the stillness. The black pony! The cry of the curlew had made me forget about him. Now it sounded as if he were trying to get up. I walked slowly towards him. Memories of being struck by that mare in the stable flooded back. My steps slowed down as I tried to conquer my fear. Nick was right. It was my fault I'd been hurt. It wasn't fair to blame all horses and ponies for my stupidity.

'How is he?' I jumped at the sound of the

low raspy voice. I hadn't heard Red Mick come up behind me.

'I thought I heard him pawing the ground,' I said. Sure enough the grass around the pony's legs was cut up.

'Ye're right. He's much improved. The heat is what he needed.'

'Will he be okay?' I asked. 'Will Mr Broderick be able to get him home?'

'I doubt Mr Broderick will be going any where except the Regional Hospital,' Red Mick answered. 'He's cut pretty bad and the bone is crushed.'

'Who will phone his family and tell them?'

'He's no family, only this ole pony. Gave up farming five or six year ago when he got the pension. He won the pony in a raffle a couple of years ago. It's all he got.'

'But who will mind him when he's in hospital?' I asked uneasily. The pony's dark eyes were watching us.

'Dunno. Guess if he's sound he'll be sold off at a fair. He's small and ain't much good for anything.'

'Will we try to get him up?' I asked.

'Leave him for a while,' advised Red Mick. 'I've got the cart fixed and the mare hitched to it. I want to get Mr Broderick loaded.'

Seeing me hesitate, he asked, 'What is it?'

'The pony... we can't leave him behind. I want to help him... but I'm afraid of him.'

I looked around, fearful of hearing that jeering laugh. But Mary was still over by the cart.

Red Mick didn't laugh. 'I know. Ye were hurt once, weren't ye? But don't be afraid. Just look at him. He's more afraid of ye than ye are of him... and if we have to leave him, we'll be back for him.'

As Red Mick headed over to Mary and the mare, I knelt down beside the pony's head and let him smell my fingers. I stroked his nose gently and whispered, 'I'm glad you're better. And I won't leave you behind. I promise.' I leaned over and let my face touch his. I felt the warmth of his skin against mine. I knew things had changed.

I slowly walked back to the mare and the cart, shivering in my damp clothes. I missed the comforting heat of the turf fire. Red Mick was adjusting the leather harness on the mare. Mary sat in the front of the cart holding the reins.

'I don't understand,' I said. 'It's still foggy. Why is it safe to go now?'

Red Mick paused and turned to me.

'Put your hand up and close yer eyes,' he said. 'What do ye feel?'

I raised both hands and closed my eyes. I couldn't feel a thing. I looked at him and shrugged.

He laughed. ''Tis a bit of a breeze coming in from the sea. It'll clear this ole fog away.'

'Are we going now?' I asked.

Mary rolled her eyes. 'Did ye forget ole Mr Broderick and his half-dead pony?' she sneered.

Why was she so cold and unfeeling? Then I remembered how her eyes had lit up when she was talking about living on the road.

'Mary, let's git this cart backed up to Mr Broderick,' Red Mick said. 'I've made a sort of board to lift him up on. The young lad and I can do that.'

We managed to lift the old man into the back of the cart, and though he grimaced with pain he seemed stronger and more alive. Red Mick padded his leg as much as he could with old fertilizer bags he had found near the reeks. Then he beckoned to me and we made our way to where the pony was lying. He gently lifted off the carpet that covered him. The sweat on his thick coat had dried in white steaks and the mud had caked. He eyed us warily from where he lay.

'Take the reins and coax him,' Red Mick said. 'I'll give him a push from behind.' Nervously I took hold of the reins, remembering how Mary had held them at the end and made little clucking noises. I did the same.

'Cluck...cluck...cluck,' I coaxed. 'C'mon, little horse, up you get.' I also remembered how Nick had always told Clare to be patient with a frightened animal. So I kept clucking and urging as gently as I could. With me lifting and Red Mick pushing from behind, the pony got himself into a crouching position.

'Good work,' Red Mick praised. 'We're

almost there. Keep coaxing.' I went on clucking and urging until finally, with a tremendous effort, the pony rose to his feet. He shook himself and snorted loudly. He was holding up one back leg.

'What's wrong with his leg?' I asked. I knew from the horses and ponies at home that lameness was a sign of injury.

'Ask him to walk a step,' Red Mick said, standing behind the pony. I clucked again and with the traveller waving his arms the pony took a reluctant step forward.

'I'd say he's caught in the hip,' Red Mick reckoned. 'The ole shafts probably bruised him. Least nothing's broke. Let's git him to walk up behind the cart.

Again, with a great deal of cajoling, we were able to lead him up to the cart. The piebald mare whinnied when she saw him approach.

Mary was watching us all the time.

'That fellah sure ain't no racehorse,' she snickered. 'But at least we won't be bringing him to the factory yard.' She gave me what I thought was a shadow of a smile and then said no more.

Just as Red Mick had predicted the heavy fog was beginning to lift, unveiling a backdrop of gathering darkness. I turned on the light of my watch. Half-past six. The fire which had been ablaze only an hour ago was now just a smouldering heap.

I looked down at the broad white stripe on the pony's face. I knew what his name would be: Blaze.

'Are ye right?' Red Mick called. He was standing in front of the mare, looking back at Mary and Mr Broderick in the cart and me leading Blaze.

'We'll take it nice and steady.' He turned and slowly led the mare forward.

12 Safe Home

Our strange procession of man and beast moved slowly along the bank of the drain. The fog had cleared. Now a full moon hung high in the cloudless sky. Red Mick led the piebald mare carefully across the sodden ground while I followed closely behind leading Blaze, who was taking short, halting steps. I prayed he wouldn't stumble and fall. What would we do with him if he did? I placed a hand on the back of the cart to steady my own feet. I had to keep up. There was no way I wanted to be left in this dark, dank swamp.

'How's he doing?' I asked Mary who was sitting beside Mr Broderick in the cart.

'I'd say he's seen better days,' she answered saucily. No wonder the teachers gave her a hard time in school; she probably deserved it.

'What are you going to do first when you get home?' I asked. 'I'm going to get Mom to make me a huge cheese pizza, then I'll change into my pyjamas, and watch telly next to the fire. What about you?'

'I'm goin' to me auntie's trailer and sit next to the range an' have a big bowl of hare stew.'

She smacked her lips dramatically. 'That is if I get home. The guards and the welfare officers are always lookin' to bring me back to the estate. They're wastin' their time. I won't stay.'

'Were you at the camp when I came on my own looking for help?' I asked her curiously.

'Brains! How else would we know to come for ye?' she retorted.

'But why didn't you come out and say something to me?' I didn't understand.

'An' chance being reported to welfare. No thanks, I've walked that road from Galway too many times. It was me grand-da who set off after ye. I snuck out after him. I had to see who was hurt.'

The wooden cart came to a halt. I recognised the spot where the grassy bank joined the bog track. We were almost to the tarred road. And home!

'Mary, hold tight to Mr Broderick,' Red Mick yelled. 'We've got to get up on the track?' The cart lurched as Gypsy strained to mount the bog track. Strangely, Mr Broderick didn't cry out. He must have fallen asleep. I tried to concentrate on getting Blaze to keep up with the cart. He had broken out in a heavy sweat again, probably due to the extra effort of hobbling on three legs.

'Does your grand-dad gripe about having you to stay?' I asked when we were moving along the track, knowing I risked being told to mind my own business.

'Nope,' she replied, 'He likes having me around. He always said if it was good enough for me ma it was good enough for me. He says I'm the image of me ma. Every way. We get on the finest.'

'Aren't you afraid of getting into trouble? I mean with the guards.' I tried to imagine myself playing cat and mouse with the guards and knew I could never do it.

'Nah!' she said casually. 'It's all a bit of a game to please me auntie in town and the school inspector. The guards know I mean no harm and me grand-da neither.'

For some odd reason the saying, 'A horse of another colour', came into my mind. Why was she so different from me?

'How long have you been at the camp?... I mean since you ran away the last time?'

'Is it two weeks or three?' She shrugged. 'Pure heaven, home on the open road.'

I asked no more questions. We were worlds apart. I looked back at Blaze as he struggled to keep up with the slow-moving cart. I thought of the horses in their warm stables at home.

Where would Blaze go, now that Mr Broderick was hurt and would have to go into hospital? Had he a home at all?

'Lights! Do ye see the lights, Red Mick.'

We all looked in the direction of my outstretched hand and saw two sets of head-lamps and a blue spinning light approaching.

'It's John, I know it's John.' I couldn't contain my excitement. 'We're going home!'

As we reached the end of the bog track, the Volvo station-wagon with a horse-box hitched to it and a Regional Hospital ambulance were waiting. Two uniformed medics ran to the cart to attend to Mr Broderick. Nick and John and another man came towards me. I could feel the tension in Blaze's reins as he shied away.

'Wait, wait there,' I called. 'The pony is hurt and very frightened.' I couldn't believe that *I* was actually saying all this. 'Steady, Blaze. Easy, boy. They're my friends, they've come to help you,' I soothed.

'Good job, Sam,' John praised. 'Keep talking to him.'

'What can we do to help?' Nick, standing beside the cart, was watching as the medics cleaned and bandaged.

'Nothing, lad,' said one of the men as the other went to fetch the stretcher. 'We just need a few details about the accident.'

I looked around for Red Mick and Mary. He stood next to Gypsy smoking a cigarette. But where was Mary? Had she gone?

'What about Blaze, I mean the pony?' I asked fearfully. 'What will happen to him?'

Red Mick said nothing. He walked over to the cart and spoke softly to Mr Broderick. A moment later he looked at me and beckoned. I reluctantly handed the pony's reins to John.

'Mr Broderick reckons he owes ye,' Red Mick began. 'He reckons ye saved his life by finding him in that drain. He feels he owes ye somethin'. A reward. He'd be grateful if ye'd take the black pony as payment. Will ye?'

I was dumbfounded. I looked at Nick. Then at John. Then at them both again.

'Can I... can I really have him?' I said in a choked voice. I leaned over the side of the cart and saw that Mr Broderick was watching me. I reached out and placed my hand in his. Was all this really happening?

'Yes, Mr Broderick,' I whispered. 'I would love to have your pony. I promise to give him a good home. Thank you, thank you.'

Red Mick gripped my shoulder and said gently, 'That ye will. That ye will.'

The medics put Mr Broderick on the

stretcher and carried him to the ambulance. Then it set off back down the tarred road.

We watched the blue spinning light until it disappeared around a bend in the road. I felt sorry for the old man who had no family. I resolved to get Mom or Dad to take me to the hospital to visit him.

'Best be pushin' on,' Red Mick said. We were still standing around the farm cart. 'Will I give ye a hand loading the small pony?'

'Good idea,' answered John smiling at me. 'He might be a handful to load.'

But between the three men and Nick he had no choice but to be coaxed and shoved into the box. I held his reins for as long as I could.

'Do you think he's badly hurt?' I asked.

'I wouldn't say so,' John replied. 'A bruised muscle more than likely. It'll be a tough job examining him. He might be small but he's strong and hearty.'

'What will Dad say?' I asked, concerned for the first time about bringing home my gift. Mom never allowed me to keep any of the stray cats or dogs that happened to wander into our yard. Dad might be worse.

'Don't mind your dad,' laughed John. 'I'll take care of him.'

'I'll be off,' Red Mick said.

'I can't thank you enough for all you did,' John said, holding out his hand. Red Mick took it and shook it. 'Here's my card. If you ever need a vet for the mare or any other pony, ring me.'

Red Mick muttered something and stuffed the card into the pocket of his stained trousers.

'Can I ask you one more thing?' I tugged gently on the traveller's jumper. 'Where's Mary? Has she gone home?'

Red Mick smiled and nodded his head. He clucked softly, holding Gypsy by the head, and they walked away.

'Come on,' said Nick, 'You've got a lot of explaining to do.' He grinned and pushed me toward the back door of the Volvo. 'I can't wait to hear what happened.'

I resisted his shove and turned toward the fading sound of Gypsy's hooves and the creaking wheels of the farm cart as it moved along the tarred road toward the travellers' camp.

I though about Mary. And the difference between us. And about poor Blaze who might have ended up in the knacker's yard. Horses of another colour?

I whispered after them. 'Safe home!'